Grandma Went to Market

Text copyright © 1995 by Stella Blackstone
Illustrations copyright © 1995 by Bernard Lodge
First American edition 1996
Originally published in Great Britain in 1995 by Barefoot Books Ltd.

Library of Congress Cataloging-in-Publication Data

Blackstone, Stella.
    Grandma went to market : a round-the-world counting rhyme / words
by Stella Blackstone; pictures by Bernard Lodge. — 1st American ed.
        p.   cm.
    Summary : Grandma travels around the world picking up items,
from one flying carpet to ten ribbons for a pony's mane, representative
of the places she visits.
    ISBN 0-395-74045-2
    [1. Voyages and travels — Fiction. 2. Geography — Fiction.
3. Counting. 4. Stories in rhyme.] I. Lodge, Bernard, ill.
II. Title.
PZ8.3.B5735Gr 1996   94-47079
[E] — dc20   CIP
                                                    AC

Printed in Italy

10 9 8 7 6 5 4 3 2 1

Grandma Went to Market

A Round-the-World Counting Rhyme

words by Stella Blackstone *pictures by* Bernard Lodge

Houghton Mifflin Company
Boston 1996

My grandma went to market
to buy a flying carpet.

She bought the flying carpet
from a man in Istanbul,
it was trimmed with yellow tassels
and made of knotted wool.

Next she went to Thailand
and flew down from the sky
to buy herself two temple cats,
Puyin and Puchai.*

*"Puyin" means little girl
"Puchai" means little boy

Then she headed westward
to the land of Mexico;
she bought three fierce and funny masks,
one red, one black, one yellow.

The flying carpet seemed to know
exactly where to take her;
they went to China next, to buy
four lanterns made of paper.*

* the symbol on the lanterns means
"double happiness."

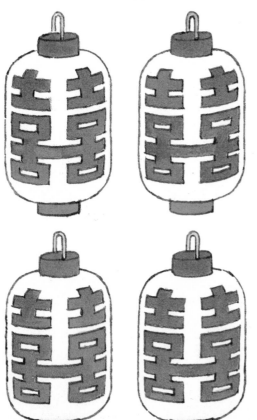

"To Switzerland!" cried Grandma
as the carpet turned around.
She bought five cowbells there, that made
a funny clanking sound.

"Now Africa!" sang Grandma.
"We must wake the morning sun!"
So they spiraled south to Kenya
where she bought six booming drums.

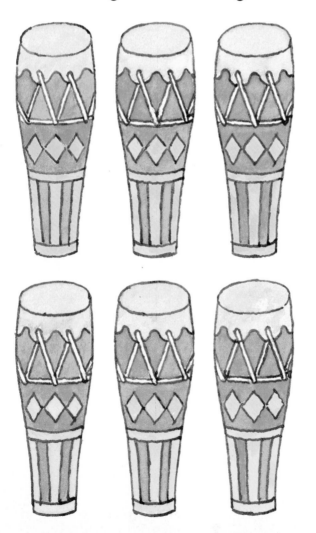

Next they traveled northward,
past the homes of mountain trolls,
to stop awhile in Russia
for seven nesting dolls.

"Australia!" Grandma ordered.
"Take me down to Alice Springs.
I want eight buzzing boomerangs
that fly back without wings."

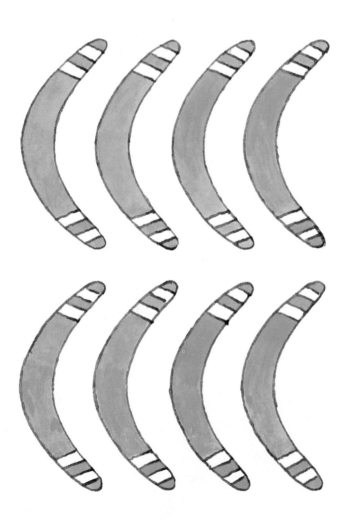

Then Grandma sighed "I've bought so much,
but nothing Japanese!"
In Tokyo she found nine kites
that fluttered in the breeze.

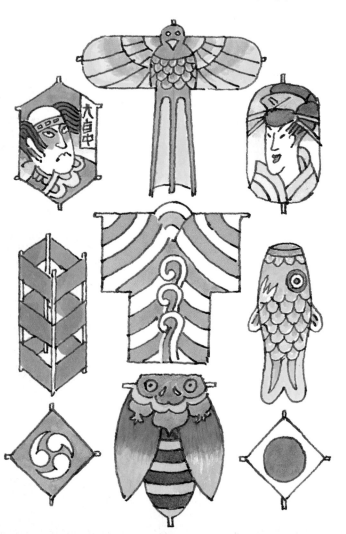

But best of all, she came back home
down Honeysuckle Lane,
where she bought me a black pony
with ten ribbons in his mane.

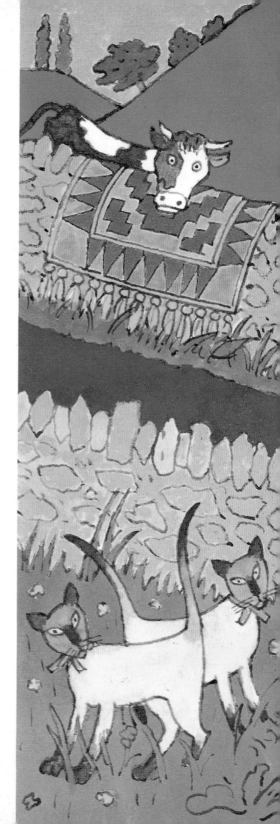

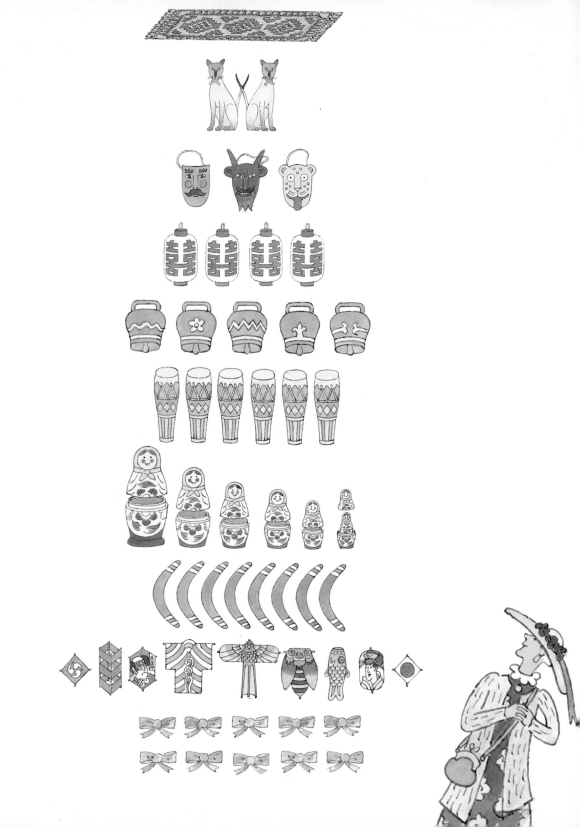